The
Flying Bath

For Felix – J.D.
For Christine Isteed – D.R.

First published 2014 by Macmillan Children's Books

a division of Macmillan Publishers Limited

20 New Wharf Road, London N1 9RR

Basingstoke and Oxford

Associated companies throughout the world

www.panmacmillan.com

ISBN: 978-0-230-74260-4

1 3 5 7 9 8 6 4 2

A CIP catalogue record for this book is available from the British Library.

Printed in China

WRITTEN BY
JULIA DONALDSON

ILLUSTRATED BY
DAVID ROBERTS

The Flying Bath

MACMILLAN CHILDREN'S BOOKS

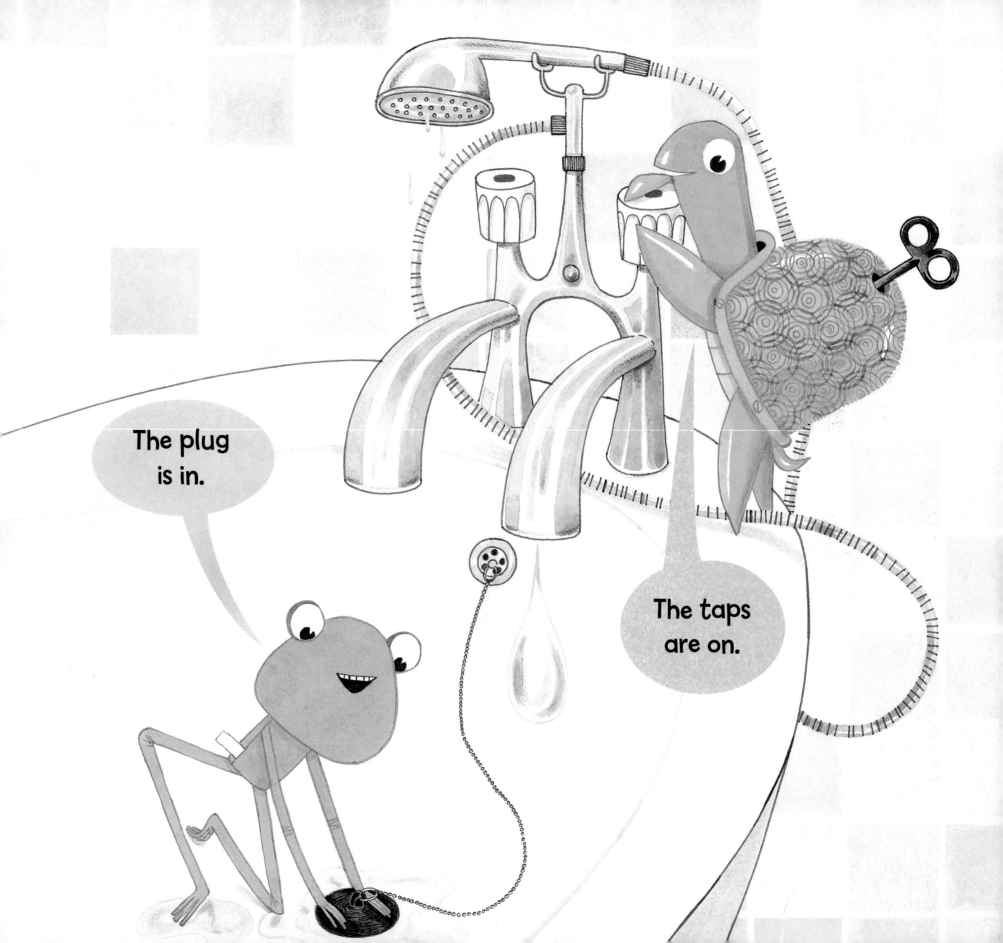

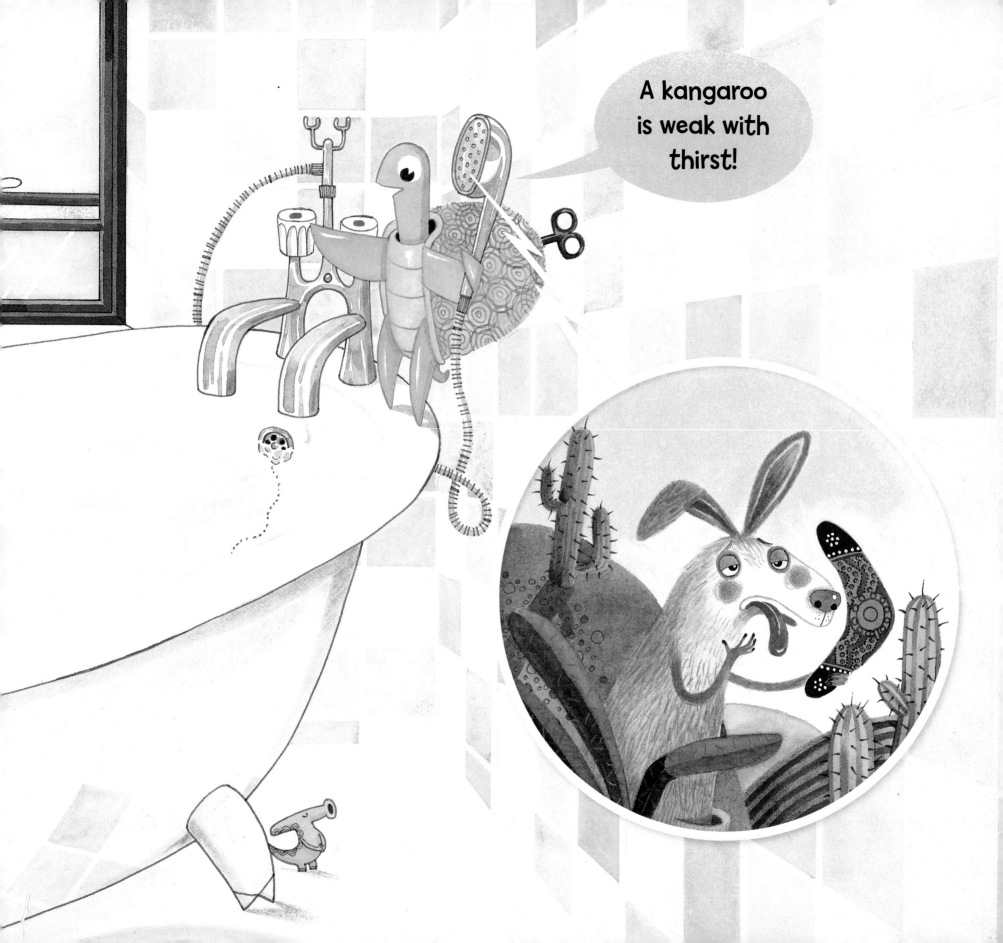

Wings out, and off we fly.
The Flying Bath is in the sky!

A bee is feeling very worried. Her flowers are droopy.

Time we hurried!

Wings out, and off we fly.
The Flying Bath is in the sky!

Thank you!
Would you like
some honey?

Yum,
yum!

Sweet and
runny!

Wings out, and off we fly.
The Flying Bath is in the sky!

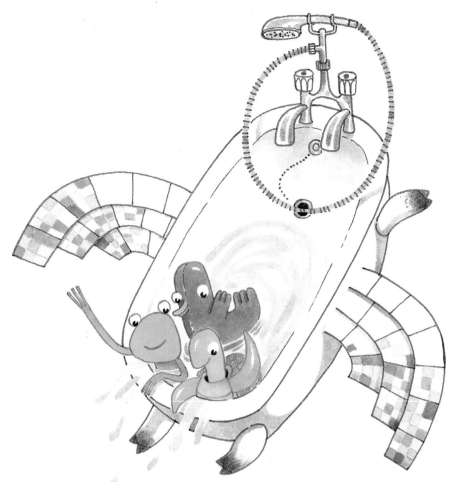

Wings out, and off we fly.
The Flying Bath is in the sky!

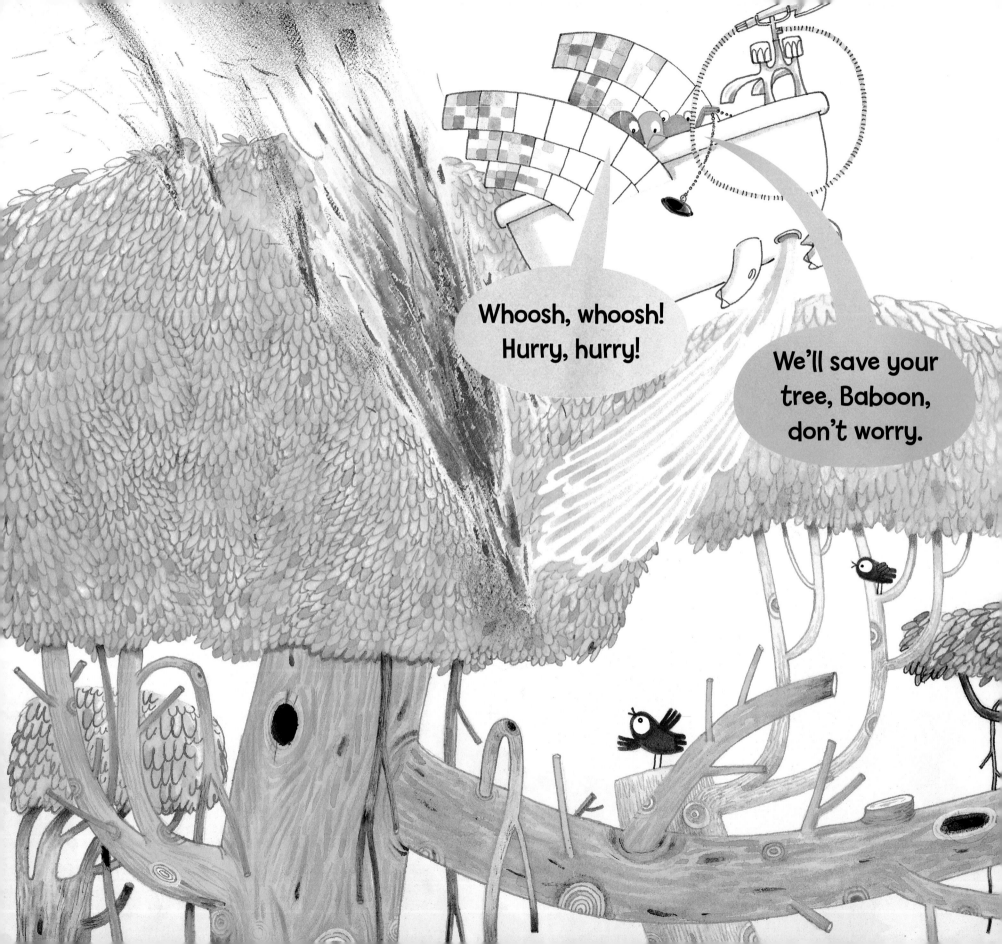

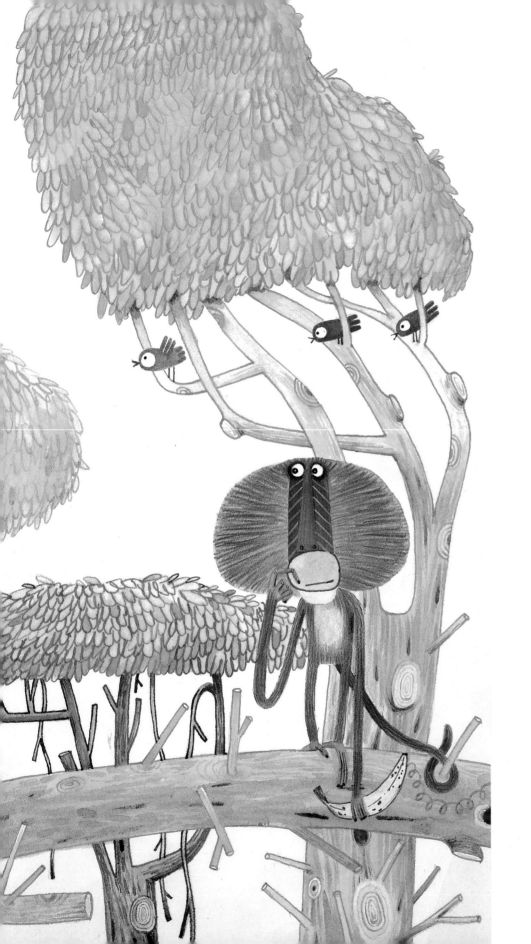

A fish is frantic.
There's a drought.
He says his pond
is drying out.

Wings out, and off we fly.
The Flying Bath is in the sky!

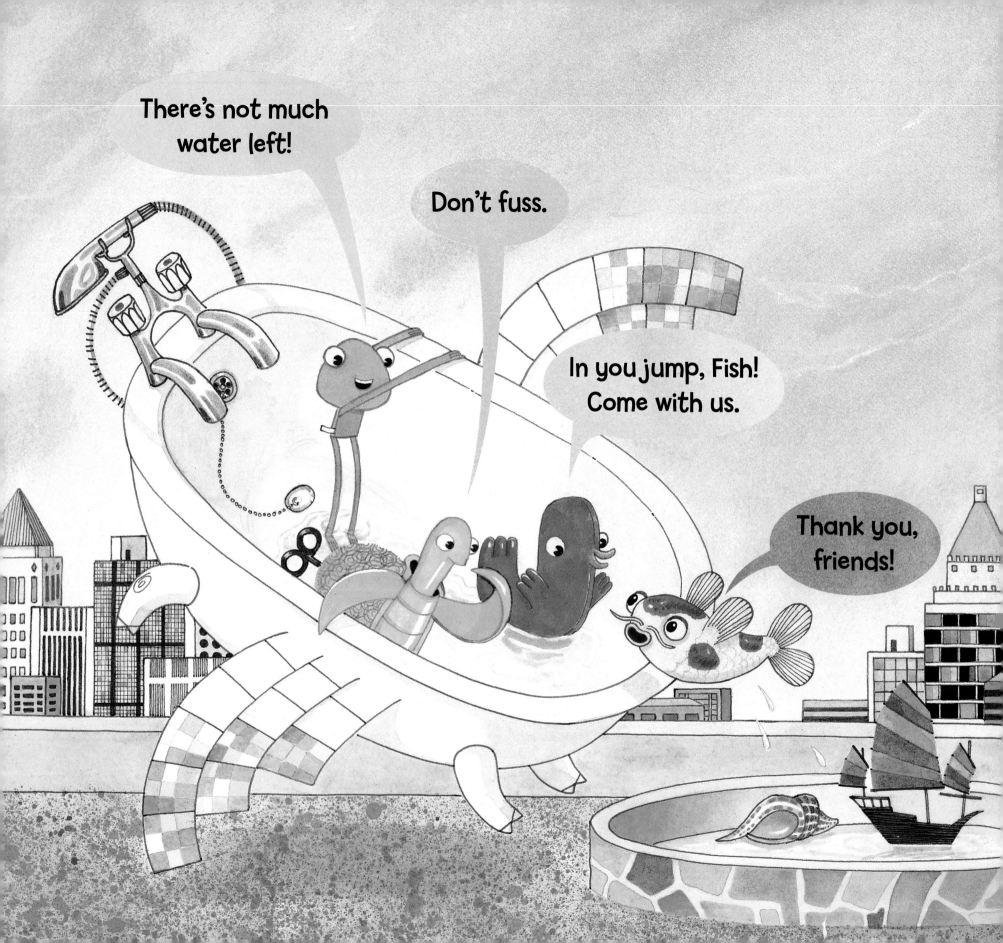

. . . but now it's late.
The Flying Bath has got a date.

Wings out, and off we fly.
The Flying Bath is in the sky!